LUCY ROSE
Here's the Thing ABOUT ME

by Katy Kelly

ILLUSTRATED BY ADAM REX

SCHOLASTIC INC.

New York Toronto London Auckland Sydney
Mexico City New Delhi Hong Kong Buenos Aires

ISBN 0-439-88432-2

Text copyright © 2004 by Katy Kelly.
Cover illustration copyright © 2004 by Adam Rex. All rights reserved.
Published by Scholastic Inc., 557 Broadway, New York, NY 10012,
by arrangement with Random House Children's Books, a division of
Random House, Inc. SCHOLASTIC and associated logos are
trademarks and/or registered trademarks of Scholastic Inc.

12 11 10 9 8 7 6 5 4 3 2 1   6 7 8 9 10 11/0

Printed in the U.S.A.   40

First Scholastic printing, September 2006

To my beloved parents,
Marguerite and Tom Kelly,
who are the real Madam and Pop
—K.K.

SEPTEMBER

September 14

Here is the thing about me: According to my dad, I am one smart cookie. And according to my grandfather, I have the kind of life that is called eventful, which means NOT boring. That is probably because my whole family is not boring, except for maybe my baby cousin, Georgie, but I don't think it's fair to judge if a person is boring until after they know how to talk. My grandmother is extremely not boring.

Here is the thing about my grandmother: She acts like her dog can tell time. When she is getting ready to go out she says, "Gumbo, I am going out to give a speech and I'll be back home at six-thirty." Then Gumbo, who is the biggest kind of black poodle you can get, clomps around making toenail noises on the hall floor. Then my grandmother says, "His behavior has been much better since I started telling him my schedule." I think this is wacko but it does tell you something about my grandmother. And just so you know, I mean wacko in a good way.

Another thing about her is that she has the exact same name as me: Lucy Rose. She is 58 and I am 8. We are both short for our age. Plus she is a writer and starting today, I am too. I am writing about my eventful life. But I am skipping the days that are not so interesting. That way there will be no dull parts.

The reason, by the way, that my grandmother makes speeches is that she is an expert on children. She has a column in the newspaper and people write her letters and ask how they can make their kids shape up and she tells them what to do. I am not a bragger so I do not tell that my grandmother is an expert but a lot of grown-ups guess, because the name of her newspaper column is "Dear Lucy Rose" and there is a picture of her at the top plus she comes to pick me up after school when my mother is working overtime. The problem with having an expert for a grandmother is that some people, when they see me doing something that she would definitely NOT recommend, like on the second day of school when I poked Adam Melon with a stick which he deserved, they tell her and then she tells my mother and then I am in for it.

When that happens my mom and I have to have a BIG CHAT and she says, "What came over you, Lucy Rose?"

Then I make my shoulders go all shruggy.

And then she says, "Let's talk about your feelings."

Then if I am in a sassy mood I say, "I am feeling like I would like to watch a little TV."

And then she says, "This is serious, Lucy Rose."

So I say, "Seriously, I am feeling fine."

And she says, "Really, Lucy Rose, tell me your true feelings."

And that conversation can go on for quite a little while.

My mother's name is Lily Reilly and she has light brown hair that is straight as string and she is five feet and one inch tall and she weighs one hundred and ten pounds exactly. She is fond of doing yoga, which is one boring sport if you ask me. Also she is an artist who works for a TV station that mostly shows the news. So a lot of times she draws maps. She would rather be an artist who draws children's books but we have a mortgage to pay. Most kids don't know about mortgages but I do because my mother is a big one for explaining things and one thing she explained is that a mortgage is how you pay for your house. "You have to send a check for it every single month," she told me. But that is A-OK with my mother because she is wild for our house.

We moved to Washington, D.C., this summer from Ann Arbor, Michigan, which is where we used to live before my parents got separated. My true feelings about that are NOT fine. They are yuck. My mom says that is to be expected but I am telling you one thing, I didn't expect it at all.

In Ann Arbor we lived in the suburbs and our house had a big yard and a garage and a family room. My dad still lives in it. He says my room will always be my room and I am glad about that because even though it still has the circus wallpaper from when I was a little kid, and even though some of it is a little peeling where I picked at it when I was supposed to be taking a nap, I feel fond of that room.

Our Washington, D.C., house is a city house. It

has a little white porch with a swing big enough for two people and a pig-shaped weather vane on the roof and no garage because when you live in the city you can walk to a lot of places and take the subway which is called the Metro. I am not one who likes waiting around for rides but I do think it's odd not having a car which we don't because my mom thinks they are expensive and not necessary. Plus, she says, if we need to drive someplace far away we can always borrow my grandparents' station wagon.

Our city backyard is puny but it has a blackberry bush and last month when it was August we got enough of those berries to make one pie big enough for two people and when it was cooked my mom and I sat on the swing and ate it all up.

At my new house I got to pick the color for my room and I picked red which my mother and my grandmother said would drive me crazy but doesn't. Plus it's original and according to my grandfather I am an original thinker.

When I talked to my dad on the phone yesterday, I told him what my grandfather said and my father told me, "It's true, Lucy Rose. You have a one-of-a-kind mind." That is a good compliment, I think.

It's because of my original thinking that I got this book that I am writing in right now. Yesterday afternoon Pop came in from a walk and gave me a little bag from the Trover Shop and inside it was this book that is red on the cover and white on the inside and on the edge is a loop that has a golden pen in it. I think most people who would get a book like this would be at least twenty years old and probably in college. Pop told me that I should write in my red book whenever I think of something that is important or funny which I do a lot of the time.

My grandparents live three blocks away from me in a three-story-tall house that my grandfather has lived in since he was born which was an extremely long time ago. It has NINE porches, some of them on the second floor that you can only get on if you climb out of the window which is something I get to do a lot because my grandmother is on a campaign against pigeons and she sends me out to stomp around and scare them away.

There are some things I like about this new neighborhood. One is that it doesn't feel brand-new on account of I've been here plenty of times

with my mom and dad to visit my grandparents. My dad says he will still come to Washington but mostly it will be to visit me.

Another good thing about this neighborhood is that it has sidewalks and you can walk to the Capitol of the United States of America which is the biggest, fanciest building ever. You can walk to the Supreme Court which has an extremely lot of steps and you can walk to Grubb's drugstore and buy Twizzlers and talk to Eddie the pharmacist which I like to do because every time he sees me he says, "What's shakin', Lucy Rose?"

And I say, "I am!" And then I shake all over like I'm going frantic.

Then Eddie says, "You've got more wiggle than a bowl full of Jell-O, Lucy Rose," which makes me crack up. Eddie has been funny his whole life. I know this because my mom and her sisters, who have the names of Aunt Marguerite and Aunt Pansy, used to work at Grubb's when they were teenagers and Grubb's had a soda fountain. It doesn't anymore because Eddie needed the space for the Beauty Aids counter.

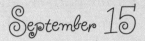

September 15

The thing about original thinkers is that they are not always so great in school but in a lot of ways I am. Considering I am in the third grade, I am excellent at drawing which is the same as my mother and fine at language arts and pretty good at making multiples with dried beans. I play the cello because I am extremely musical which is like my dad who was a French horn player when he was in his high school marching band and it was the best band in the whole state of Michigan. I am not kidding. They won a trophy for it. And I am probably the best at morning greetings which is a credit to my grandmother because she is very big on greetings and has been rather firm that I should be too. A lot of kids don't know that you should look a grown-up right in the eyes when you meet them and you should say something pleasant and call them by their name. Also you should be thankful if they give you something, even if it is gross. I learned this when my great-aunt Ginnie sent me a green sweater that itched and had too long sleeves for my birthday and I did not feel thankful at all but my grandmother said, "Lucy Rose, a person's taste can change overnight and the next time you might get lucky."

That has not happened to me so far but I take her recommendations because she is from New Orleans and that is one polite city.

September 16

Here is one good thing: Today I got a postcard from my dad and on the front is a picture of a kid fishing and it says, "I thought I'd drop you a line!" On the back it says Miss Lucy Rose Reilly, which sounds older than 8, I think. Also there is a note that says: "Dear Lucy Rose, I hope your new school is swell. Is it? I love you, Dad."

My dad is a teacher of history at Ann Arbor Junior High School so he is one who wants to know every last thing about my school.

I made a postcard back. My grandmother gave it to me. It is not so interesting on the front because it just has a picture of the Lincoln Memorial which you can see anytime you want if you look at a penny.

On the other side of the card, I wrote my old address and my dad's name and I called him Mr. Bob Reilly. Next to that I wrote: "Dear Dad, It's okay, I guess."

That was not the whole, exact truth.

September 22

One hard part about being an original thinker is that sometimes it makes teachers glare at you and Mrs. Washburn is a big one for glaring. Also she likes people to "STAY SEATED" just about all the time. When I explained about her at dinner last night, my grandfather said, "Mrs. Washburn doesn't have an original bone in her whole body."

Then my mom said, "It's only September and she might get better in a month or two." Which I doubt.

Luckily Mrs. Washburn is only a two-morning-a-week teacher who comes to help with reading.

My everyday teacher is Mr. Welsh and he does not glare. Today he came up to me at lunch and he said, "How are you settling in, Lucy Rose?"

And I said, "Okie-dokie."

And he said, "That's great."

And I said, "Well, a little okie-dokie."

"Only a little?" he asked me.

I told him, "Actually, it is not the easiest to be the new kid in the neighborhood and the new kid at school at the exact same time especially when you don't know any friends yet."

He had sympathy for that because he told me, "I had a hard time when I was a new teacher and I didn't know any of the other teachers or any of the kids and, to tell you the truth, the principal made me a little nervous, but after a while it got better."

"Are you still nervous of the principal?"

"Nope," he said. "But it took a little time for me to get the hang of everything. I think that will be true for you, too."

"Doubt it," I said.

"Lucy Rose," Mr. Welsh said, "I'll eat my hat if things don't get better for you next month."

I have never seen him wear a hat so he might be kidding but I hope he is not because it is almost October and that is the next month and I would really like it to be better.

Here are some things about Mr. Welsh: He has a nice look of not too much hair and little round eyeglasses and he is skinnier than my dad and my grandfather, probably because he is one for good eating habits. Plus he has two daughters who are in junior high and a son who is still a kid and a wife who works at the organic store. Mr. Welsh is a big one for jokes. Also palindromes, which are words that are spelled the same forwards and backwards. I know about them from my father and so far I have six. One of them is Dad. I told Mr. Welsh another one which is the girl name of Eve. And he said, "You have a way with palindromes, Lucy Rose."

And I said, "Yes, I absolutely do because I'm the one that figured out that we should call my grandmother Madam and my grandfather Pop."

"What did you used to call them before?" Mr. Welsh asked me.

"We called my grandmother Grandma but she likes Madam better."

"How come?" he asked me.

"She says it makes her feel rich and she says who wouldn't like that?" I told him. "And we always did call Pop, Pop, it's just that in the beginning I didn't know he was a palindrome."

Mr. Welsh is an original thinker.

OCTOBER

There are some things I like about school and some things I don't. One that I do is my table which is really four desks pushed together. Jonique McBee sits at my table and she is very beautiful and has pierced ears which is a dream of mine and she has a zippering pencil case with purple tassels and her best thing is math. She doesn't talk very much, but on Monday she did tell me that she thinks freckle faces are pretty which was a pleasing thing to say to me since I have that kind of face exactly. So I said, "I wish I had the kind of hair that can have lots of braids and lots of barrettes," which is the kind she has exactly.

And she said, "I like hair that is red like yours."

So I said, "I get it from my father."

I did not tell that he lives in Ann Arbor.

And then she said, "When I get older I am going to get a retainer."

And I said, "You are the luckiest duck ever."

Also at my table there is a boy named Bart Bigelow who picks his nose which is something you are way too old to do in third grade but he does it anyway and then he wipes it on his jeans which is so gross and disgusting that I know already that no matter how old he gets he will never get a wife because that is not the sort of thing grown ladies stand for. But for now he is making me gag, which is another palindrome. The other person at our table is Sam Alswang and he is so funny he could be on TV. One thing that we do is change tables every so many weeks. I don't know why.

Also in our class we have a table with fish fossils that came from about a million years ago and animal teeth that came from the National Zoo on Connecticut Avenue because Mr. Welsh has a friend that works in Small Mammals.

And we have a small mammal that's a guinea pig named Jake but he is not on the table. He is in a cage. He is four and he has all his teeth and I am wild for him like anything, partly because he is cute in the face but also because of his personality which is extremely excellent, especially considering he can't talk. If you call out "Jake" he won't

turn around. That is probably because Mr. Welsh lets every class pick a new name. Last year his name was Bubba and the year before that he was named Sheila and the year before that he was named Nick after Nick at Nite. When he is sleeping he looks like a wig.

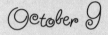

October 9

Yesterday we learned a poem about fourteen hundred and ninety-two when Columbus sailed the ocean blue and Mr. Welsh said that Christopher Columbus is such an important guy for discovering America that we get off from school because of him and that his holiday is coming on next Monday and when Mr. Welsh said that I felt like I had to talk to him right that minute and I got up from my chair and ran to his desk and he said, "Lucy Rose, do you have an emergency?"

And I said, "Yes."

And he said, "What is it?"

And I said, "Can I take Jake home for the three-day weekend of Columbus's Day?"

And he said, "No."

So I said, "But otherwise he will starve to death."

And Mr. Welsh said, "Lucy Rose, Jake will be fine because he is going to stay with Kathleen Sullivan."

And then he said I should go back to my table and sit down so the class could do some more talking about Christopher Columbus.

I already knew about him and his boat and his holiday from second grade so I double did not care.

October 11

One handy thing about my grandparents is that they are both writers and they are the kind of writers who work at home. When I am in school Madam writes "Dear Lucy Rose" in her office upstairs and Pop writes stories for magazines in his office downstairs and when it is lunchtime they meet in the kitchen and Madam tries to get him to like eating tofu. Most days I am at their house from after school until my mother comes to get me and that is pretty fun most of the time.

Today after school Pop and I took Gumbo for a walk to the Lustre Cleaners so we could pick up

Madam's speech-making dress and Pop asked me, "What is on your mind, Lucy Rose?"

One funny thing about Pop is that he can always tell when my mind has something on it. I told him about Kathleen getting to take care of Jake. "It is not fair because she already has a dog plus a parakeet plus a baby brother and I have not one living thing," I said.

"I guess the problem is that there are a lot of kids and only one guinea pig," Pop told me.

And I said, "For the first two weeks of school we had two but Jake kept fighting him so Mr. Welsh sent the other one that has the name of Wilson down to live in the kindergarten room with Miss Freeman which seems all right to me because she is one agreeable lady. Yesterday when I stepped on Adam Melon's sandwich I had to spend recess in Miss Freeman's room and she helped me clean the Nutella off my cowgirl boot. She also did not ask me if I did it on purpose, which I appreciated."

Pop made the noise of "Hmmm."

"Adam Melon," I said, "is one big problem."

"How big?" Pop asked.

"Gigantic huge," I said. "He has been bothering

me since even before the first day of school when we both had to visit our classroom ahead of time to meet Mr. Welsh on account of we're both new. Only he came to live in Washington because his father works for a congressman from Florida which he thinks is a hot-stuff job, which it is, but I don't tell him that because he would just brag more than he does already."

"No," Pop said. "You don't want to encourage a boy like that."

"No, I don't," I said. "But ever since that visiting day he keeps chasing me when I don't want to be chased plus he said I had a stupid lunch which is why I stepped on his."

One good thing about Pop is he is not an over-reactor. "He said you had a stupid lunch, did he?" Pop asked me, skipping right over the stepping-on part.

"Sorry to say he was right," I said. "My mom doesn't approve of Chee-tos and she buys fake Oreos to save money plus she makes roll-ups with turkey and cheese which are embarrassing."

"Maybe Madam could make your lunch some-times," Pop said.

"Even worse," I said. "She is crazy for lentil salad and also soy bars."

Pop said he has sympathy for that because he himself is no fan of soy foods.

When we got back to my grandparents' house I sat around in Madam's office while she typed her answer to a lady who e-mailed about her teenager daughter who dillydallies with her homework and then has to stay up until midnight to finish it and then she doesn't want to get up in the morning so they are always late for school and then the whole carpool gets tardy on their report cards. Instead of writing her name at the bottom of the letter the lady called herself Frustrated in Franconia. I asked Madam, "How come she doesn't say her name?"

"Sometimes people are too embarrassed to tell me their real name," Madam said. "And sometimes I suspect a letter comes from someone I know but they want privacy so they don't use their real name."

"Oh," I said. "What did you tell Frustrated to do?"

"I told her to make her daughter go to bed on time even if her homework isn't done because that is the way to cure dillydallying fast."

Pop came into Madam's office right when I was telling Madam, "I know about being frustrated because of Adam Melon chasing me every minute."

And she said, "He might be doing that because he likes you."

"Man-o-man," I said. "That is dumb."

"True," Madam said. "But that's what boys do sometimes."

Then I said, "In my brain I call him Melonhead."

Madam said that is rude but Pop said it's funny. Then Madam said, "Lucy Rose, what you need to do is make a good friend and then maybe Adam Melon won't seem so important."

To which I said "Poop" which is, by the way, a palindrome. Like I said, Madam is one for advice.

October 18

Even though I had decided to skip Madam's recommendation I changed my mind this morning when I was at school. Mrs. Washburn was reading out loud about the house on the prairie but I did not feel in a mood to listen to that book. I was thinking about how October was supposed to be better and how it actually isn't.

Later, when I was supposed to be doing nouns, I wrote a list on the back of my language arts work-sheet called WHAT MY NEW FRIEND SHOULD BE:

1. Funny.
2. An original thinker.
3. Doesn't like Melonhead.

I took it home and showed my list to everybody at family dinner.

"Those are three important things," Pop said.

But Madam told me, "You might want to think about it some more."

Then my mom said, "Lucy Rose, you should give kids a chance and try to be friendly and ask them about themselves."

And then all of a sudden, right there in Madam and Pop's dining room, I shouted at everybody, "I am sick of school and I want to go home to Ann Arbor where I already have friends!"

I didn't expect to say it. It just came out and I'm not even sure it's all the way true.

"Well," Pop said, "you have a point about school. I used to tell your mother and her sisters and brother, 'School is as close to prison as I hope you children ever come.'"

Then Madam gave him her sharp look and said "Not helpful" in a whispery way which I could hear.

So my grandfather said, "I just don't think people should have to go inside when a bell rings or have to go outside just when they might be doing something interesting."

My mom says my grandfather has never been one for taking too much direction. I say that is a sign of an original thinker.

After dinner we walked to Grubb's and I got a lime Popsicle out of the Igloo freezer which are not as good as Good Humors but it is fun to hang your head down in the box while you are looking. And I used my own quarter to buy a postcard with a picture of the Capitol on the front to send to my Ann Arbor friends who are twins and have the names of Frannie and Annie Rhineburger. Also at Grubb's my grandfather bought a box of white Tic Tacs, which is the only kind I like, and told me I could carry them around in my pocket which is good because one thing I am big on is fresh breath.

October 23

Here is one good thing: Halloween is coming. I am going to be Annie from *Annie Get Your Gun* which is a play on Broadway which is in New York City and even though I have never been to New York City I know all the songs because we have the CD which my dad bought me because I am crazy for show tunes.

The bad thing is that I am really Annie DON'T Get Your Gun because my mother says carrying pistols is not appropriate. But she did take me to buy a red cowgirl hat at the Bruce Variety and also a shirt with fringe and pearly snap buttons. I'm also going to wear a blue jean skirt I already have and my same red cowgirl boots that I wear every day. And here is the thing of it: I look divine.

This is another good thing: Jonique's mother called up my mother and said that since they live on A Street and we live one block away on Third

Street that I can come trick-or-treating with them. The bad thing: Melonhead is coming too. Jonique says he has to. His mother asked. At lunch Jonique gave me three Doritos and I gave her so many Tic Tacs I didn't even count. White are the only kind she likes too.

October 28

I am not a complainer but it is only three days until October is over so when I got to school this morning I told Mr. Welsh flat out that he had to eat his hat.

"How come?" he said.

"Things are not better this month," I told him.

"Not even a little bit?" he said.

"Maybe a puny bit," I said.

"There are still a few days left," he said. "Look for the good, Lucy Rose."

"Right-O," I said but I did not really go for that advice.

"Good. I'm rather fond of my hat," he said.

Which I have still never seen him wearing.

NOVEMBER

November 1

Yesterday was Halloween and it was extremely excellent. Mr. Welsh dressed up like a bunch of grapes with purple balloons all over himself which was hilarious and when one popped he jumped like a rocket.

After lunch the whole school had a costume parade starting with the kindergarteners and we marched around the block and all of the old people who are living at the Capitol Hill Home came out and waved at us and my mom ran ahead and took a video and Madam and Pop clapped like crazy and afterwards we all went back to the classroom and had a party and the best thing at the party was orange pumpkin cupcakes and they were made by my mom. Mr. Welsh ate one even though he says he is not one for eating sweets.

When we got home my mom made me eat string cheese for protein and then she went to work for the late shift and at five o'clock Pop and Madam and Gumbo walked me over to Jonique's and guess what? Her mother is a holiday nut. Their whole porch was covered with pretend spiderwebs and their doormat screams when you step on it and we drank orange Kool-Aid and ate green spaghetti which Mrs. McBee said were monster brains but were so fake. Jonique was dressed up like a jack-in-the-box with a clown hat on her head and a big red box around her middle that had a turning thing that really turned and Mrs. McBee made the whole costume herself and when I saw it I said, "Mrs. McBee, you are a genius!" And she and Mr. McBee laughed like crazy at that. I don't know why.

A girl named Asia that lives next door to the McBees came with us and she was dressed up like *I Dream of Jeannie*, which is one TV show I am crazy about. Melonhead came too and I was not thrilled about that. He was dressed like a pirate but didn't look so different than normal. Mrs. McBee stayed home to wear her witch hat and give out Skittles and Mr. McBee took us around the block, past the Faith Tabernacle church and down East Capitol Street and in front of Grubb's which was closed.

For trick-or-treating the girls all walked together and Mr. McBee walked a few houses back from us but right there one little step behind us for the whole night was Melonhead, following us around and making fart noises, which by the way is something that sends Madam right around the bend.

"Just ignore him," Jonique said.

So I yelled back, "We are ignoring you."

And Asia said, "We can't hear you."

And I held my nose and so did Asia but Jonique couldn't on account of her costume made it so she couldn't reach her nose.

But Melonhead kept right on doing it all night long.

After we got back to Jonique's house, her mother took Polaroid pictures of all of us standing on the porch under a giant spiderweb and then she gave us each a picture to take home. I was thinking about asking her if she would make me two pictures, so I could keep one and send one to my dad, but I didn't because for one thing: I didn't want to act greedy. And for another thing: I didn't want to explain about being separated. Plus it's not the most valuable picture because it has Melonhead in it. When I got back home I was going to cut him off but my mom says you can't cut Polaroids so now I have a picture

of him right there in my room. I also have an enormous lot of candy with no Baby Ruths because I hate them and I traded them to Asia for Twix bars. And I have a big pile of black licorice because both Asia and Jonique hate it so they gave it to me for free on account of I like it a teensy bit. And I have no Mounds bars which I also hate but Madam loves like anything so today after school I went to my grandparents' house and gave them to her. We went into the kitchen and Madam got apple juice for me and fizzy water for herself and Pop, and I told Madam, "I took your recommendation but Melonhead is still a big pain in my butt."

And Madam made a little smile but she told me, "You can probably think of a better way to say that."

And then my grandfather said, "I can."

But my grandmother said, "Please don't."

She is a big one for saying please.

November 2

Today I told Mr. Welsh to hold off on eating his hat and he asked me why and I said, "Because October got better in the nick of time."

"Much better?" he asked me.

"Some better," I said.

"That's a lucky break for me, hat-wise," he said. "Want to go double or nothing?"

I asked him, "What does that mean?"

And he said, "I'll bet November will be even better."

"Twice as better?" I asked.

"I think so," he said.

One thing I hope is that he is right.

November 5

Today we had an assembly and a real scientist came to the auditorium and did demonstrations and they were not the boring kind. First he made foam and then he showed us disappearing ink which was amazing like you couldn't believe and then he said, "This magical ink is made from an ordinary household object. Who can guess the ingredient?"

And then he pointed at me and I said, "Window cleaner!"

"Good try," he said. "But wrong answer."

Then Sam guessed, "Soap mixed with regular ink!"

Then Melonhead shouted out, "Lemon juice."

And he did it without even waiting to be called on.

And the man said, "You're right!" Then he told Melonhead to come up to the stage and take a bow because he has been to a lot of auditoriums and Melonhead was the first kid that ever guessed. And when Melonhead got up onstage, he bowed and then he did a dance and made hooty noises. And I have to tell you that made me feel a little steaming.

When I told my mom about that she said, "Well, Adam does know a lot about science."

"It's not the science I mind," I told her. "It's the showing off."

November 10

Here is a good thing: Three days ago my mom got a new computer on account of we left our old one in Ann Arbor for my dad. We set it up on a little desk in the kitchen and my mom said, "We have to pick a screen name for our e-mail."

And I said, "I think lilyandlucyrose would be good."

"Too long," my mom said and then she started laughing over her idea. "Since we're a lily and a rose, we could be flowerpower."

And I said, "Outstanding." So we are flowerpower and that is excellent because it is like having a spy name and nobody will know it is us unless we tell them.

So now every day when I get home I check e-mail and see if there is one for me and there usually is and it is usually from my dad. This is what he wrote to me today:

"Knock-knock."

"Who's there?"

"Olive."

"Olive who?"

"Olive you!"

I didn't get it until I said the whole thing out loud. Then I made an e-mail back and it said: "Olive you 2." Sometimes I am just plain hilarious.

When I showed it to my mom, she made a print-out of the whole thing and I taped it to the wall in my room.

November 11

This morning I asked my mother to get me to school before any of the other kids so I could ask

Mr. Welsh a private question. And she said, "Care to share?"

And I said, "Nope. 'Cause it's private."

I am not telling her because I want it to be a surprise.

After she dropped me off I waited on the steps in the freezing and the minute I saw him I ran up and said, "Hey, Mr. Welsh, can I please keep Jake for Thanksgiving vacation?"

And he said, "I'm sorry, Lucy Rose. I already promised Robinson Gold that she could do it."

And before I even could ask my next question he said that Jake was going to spend winter break with the Kempner sisters on account of it was their guinea pig that had born Jake in the first place.

I do not think this is fair. Later, when I got to my grandparents' house, I explained it to Pop and he agreed with me. When I told Madam she did not say unfair but she did say, "If Jake can't spend the night, maybe Jonique can."

And I said, "That is one idea I can go for."

So she got right on the phone to Mrs. McBee and had a chat and Mrs. McBee said this weekend would be fine.

Plus, I told Madam, it's smart. I already spend Friday nights at my grandparents' because my mother has to work the overnight, which means she doesn't get home until *Wake Up Washington* is over and then she needs her sleep but seriously.

November 15

Finally it is Friday and right after school, Jonique and I ran to her house and packed her best pajamas that are pink and white striped and her slippers that look like her feet are inside of white cats and then we ran double-fast to Madam and Pop's house. Madam gave us dried apricots for a snack and I took Jonique to the creepy basement where there used to be a kitchen in the really olden days. I showed her the best thing of all and it is the dumbwaiter which is a wooden box with a rope that works like an elevator and in the olden days used to send food from the basement up to the dining room which is on the first floor and we practiced sending our apricots up and down and then we left them in the dumbwaiter because Jonique says dried apricots are P-U.

Then I showed her the little room that is

practically full of picture frames and she said, "How come?"

"Because Madam buys them at yard sales," I told her.

And then Jonique said, "Why does she do that?"

"Because she's going to do something with them one day," I said.

"I'd like to see what," Jonique said, which I think shows she's got curiosity which is something else Pop admires and original thinkers are full of.

After that we went upstairs so she could look at the morning room, which is where Madam and Pop like to sit every morning and read the *Washington Post* newspaper and drink Red Zinger tea.

And then we went into the living room and my grandfather turned on the chandelier that has fire instead of lightbulbs and is left over from before lightbulbs were even invented.

Then I showed her the big stairs in the front hall and the little stairs in the back hall which are small and bendy and feel like a secret passageway even though they're not and we pretended we were spies making a big escape.

Then we went to my grandparents' bedroom so we

could loll around on the chaise for a while. Jonique never heard of a chaise before so I told her, "A chaise is kind of like a sofa, only fancier because it has a curvy back."

When we were done we looked into my grandmother's closet. Madam has a love of clothes and high heels and also hats which she wears when she has to do something that makes her feel nervous. She says wearing a hat makes her feel more take-charge and that is helpful when you are a short lady like she is. Jonique tried on Madam's big straw hat with soft pink and red roses and I tried on a little smoothy black one with a veil. "You look like a movie star," I told Jonique.

And she said, "That is true. I do. And you look like a famous singer."

So I stood at the top of the big steps and sang "When the Moon Hits Your Eye Like a Big Pizza Pie" and Jonique kept shouting, "Bravo!" so I sang the encore of "Sit Down, You're Rockin' the Boat" which comes from the musical of *Guys and Dolls* which is one of the best shows ever. I know because when we lived in Ann Arbor my mom and dad and I saw it at a matinee at the Ann Arbor Junior

High School and I loved that afternoon a lot.

Then we went down the front stairs by sliding down the banister for a shortcut and I showed her my grandfather's study which is absolutely full to the extreme of books and interesting things including a picture of my mother when she was two years old standing next to a chimpanzee who is wearing roller skates and my mother is crying. Pop says she was jealous of the monkey which was a shame since my grandfather, who used to be a newspaper reporter, went to a lot of trouble to borrow it from a circus man he was writing a story about and I say I wish we still had that monkey. Also in his office is a picture of Madam when she was nineteen years old, dressed up like a racing jockey sitting on a horse and boy, is she young looking and I think that would be a good picture to put at the top of "Dear Lucy Rose." Plus there are a lot of lion statues in there because Pop's best friend, that has the name of Uncle Bobo, gives them to him every birthday because Pop has the horoscope of Leo and Leos are proud like lions and also willful and actually I am a Leo too. That means we both have our birthdays in August. I almost wasn't a Leo because I was supposed to come in

September but I was born three weeks early. That is lucky for me because if I was born that one puny month later I would miss the cutoff day and I'd have to be in second grade, not third. But instead it just means I am the youngest person in my class.

Finally I showed Jonique my room which is back upstairs and is nice but not red because my grandmother would not go for it in her house. To make my room real interesting, I pretended I was a tour guide and pointed at the bed. "This is a quilt that came from an estate sale," I said. "And over here we have a doll carriage that used to be my mom's when she was six and this is a lamp that came from Mexico when Madam and Pop were on a honeymoon."

"Your grandparents must be rich," Jonique said.

But I told her they aren't. "It's just when my grandfather's parents bought this house mortgages were plenty cheaper than they are now."

Before Jonique came over I asked my grandmother to please cool it with the lentils partly for taste and partly because whenever we have them Pop sings a dopey song called "I'm Just Keen About a Bean" which I didn't think would be the best thing on Jonique's first time of sleeping over. So Madam did cool it and we had beef stew which was okay if you skipped the carrots. After dinner when Jonique and I were clearing the table, she whispered in my ear, "I was wishing for chicken fingers."

I had to tell her, "That is one wasted wish as far as my grandparents go. The only time they ever even went to McDonald's was when their house was getting painted."

"That's all?" she asked me.

"In their whole lives," I said.

But that is not a complaint because after dinner we got to make sidewalk sundaes which my grandmother invented and you get to put Hershey's syrup and marshmallows and peanuts in an ice cream cone and then fill it up with strawberry ice cream plus more chocolate syrup and coconut and sprinkles and a cherry on top and then eat it outside because it is messy like you wouldn't believe and you have to wash your hands with the hose before you can come back inside and even though it makes you shivery, it's worth it. When she finished it, Jonique told Madam, "That was the best ice cream cone I ever ate." And that was a pleasing thing to hear.

After that we had our showers and got in our PJs and we tried to put my old nightgown on Gumbo which would have been hilarious but he was not cooperating. At nine o'clock we went to bed but since we were not tired we got right up again to have a visit with my grandparents who were in their bed, which is called a four-poster and is very high and has a canopy roof on top. They were reading their books and Pop was wearing red lady-looking eyeglasses with one of the sides missing and Madam was wearing little black glasses that have a safety pin on one corner. This made Jonique laugh and I showed her that my grandparents keep a whole basket full of eyeglasses on their night table. "Since they wear the same exact prescription they just wear whatever ones they pick up first," I told her.

"My mom only has one pair of glasses," Jonique said.

"That is such an admirable quality in a person," Madam said. "But we misplace ours every five minutes so now we just buy a lot at the Price Club."

And then later when Jonique and I were under the estate sale quilt in my room in the dark and you could hear the pigeons on my porch, Jonique said, "Mrs. Washburn gets on my very last nerve."

And I said, "Mine too." Then I told her that I call Adam Melon Melonhead in my mind.

"That is hilarious," she said and then she laughed so hard she snorted.

And then we were quiet for a while and I thought Jonique might be asleep but then I thought she might not so I said, "Hey, Jonique."

And she said, "Hey, Lucy Rose."

And I said, "Here's a thing about me: My parents got a separation so now my dad doesn't live with us."

"That's what I already figured out," Jonique said.

"You did?" I said. "How come you didn't say anything?"

"Because I thought it would make you sad," she said.

"Sometimes it does," I told her.

November 18

On the next Monday I got an e-mail from my dad and it said: "Hello, L.R., BBBBBBBBBB. See Bees. Get it? Dad."

See Bees is the first two-word palindrome I ever heard of. My dad is smart like I can't believe. It comes from being a teacher, I think. I e-mailed back the palindrome of "Wow."

And he wrote back "XOX" for one hug and two kisses and also for another palindrome.

November 22

A good thing is that instead of having New Words today we got to make Pilgrim people out of dried leaves that you peel off of corn on the cob. The greatest thing was that the teacher for Pilgrim people was Mrs. McBee. Man-o-man, was I surprised. She was wearing turkey earrings and carrying a big box of stuff and then she said, "I need a volunteer."

And I called out, "Pick me! Pick me, Mrs. McBee!"

And she did pick and it was me and I got to stand up in front and be in charge of the gluing for the demonstration of making Pilgrim bodies. And then Jonique got to glue the eyes on the Pilgrim man and Sam got to help make the Pilgrim lady and

Melonhead didn't get to be a volunteer at all and I will tell you privately, his Pilgrim wasn't so hot looking.

November 23

Today I had a very tricky idea. When my mom was in the shower I made an e-mail letter to DearLucyRose@goodadvice.com. And here is what it said: "Dear Lucy Rose, Do you know any way to get a man and a lady who are separated to go back together?" I signed it "From Someone You Don't Know" and I clicked on SEND.

November 24

I got an answer from my "Dear Lucy Rose" e-mail and here is what Madam wrote: "Dear Someone I Don't Know, When people get separated the people who love them best usually wish they would go back to being a couple. Kids wish this especially— not that I am saying you are a kid—but the truth is that there is not a way."

That is not what I call good advice.

November 26, Thanksgiving Day

Our Thanksgiving dinner is always at Madam and Pop's but all of the other years of my whole life my mom and dad and I got there by plane. This year my mom and I walked over in the morning and right away Madam gave us the job of making pies. Pecan is Madam's best pie and pumpkin is Pop's so we made both of them and while we were waiting for them to cook my mom opened the bottle of vanilla extract and put some on her finger and rubbed it behind our ears for perfume and Pop said we smelled delicious. Then my mom and I cooked the cranberry sauce and Madam made mashed parsnips which aren't so bad and Pop cooked the turkey because that is his number one cooking job every year and we all set the table with Madam's plates that you have to be really careful with because they came from her old aunt. Madam had a big bowl of yellow flowers for the table but when I gave her the Pilgrim people she said they were the best decorations ever so we put the flowers on the little table in the hall and the Pilgrims on the big table with us.

Before we ate we all held hands and Madam said, "I am thankful to have my daughter and granddaughter so close by."

My grandfather said, "I am thankful to be in the bosom of my family," which is a very embarrassing word and I don't know why Madam didn't say something considering she thinks "butt" is so terrible.

My mother said, "I am thankful for new beginnings."

I said, "I am thankful for one good friend named Jonique McBee."

And then I figured out that this month things did get better.

DECEMBER

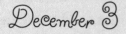

Firstly, it is changing table time at school and now Jonique is all the way over by the supply closet and I am near the front, which I happen to know from the lunch aide is where Mr. Welsh puts talkers. The good thing is I have Pierra Kempner at my table and she is a kind of girl who is fun plus almost all her clothes and her sneakers and her coat are purple which Jonique and I think is cool but which our mothers would never go for. And I have Emily Kate and she is like my grandfather says: a good egg. But here's the really bad worst news: Right across from me is Melonhead. And all day long he kept flicking paper bits at me and I stared at him hard and mean so he would know to CUT IT OUT but he didn't. So finally I told him to STOP IT and Mr. Welsh told me to SETTLE DOWN and he didn't want to hear about the paper bits.

But even that is not the biggest thing I am thinking about. The biggest thing is that I have a problem that, like Madam says, is looming large, which means is extremely big and on your mind a lot, and it is Jake. So when I got home from school today I asked Madam to make me a recommendation on how to get a turn with that guinea pig. But at that minute she was working on answering a problem question for "Dear Lucy Rose" from a lady who has a daughter who has tantrums to get stuff that she wants. The lady said she is at her wits' end plus she is embarrassed every time they go to a store and she was Fed Up in Friendship Heights. I told Madam that my recommendation would be that the lady should say "FORGET IT" and BE FIRM about it and Madam said that was about the right answer but that her editor needs two hundred and fifty words so she would have to stretch it out. She said we would talk about my problem at dinner.

But at dinner my mother said, "This is news to me, Lucy Rose. You never mentioned wanting to bring Jake home."

"That's because it was supposed to be a surprise," I said.

And then she made a big confession that she was

not wild for rodents and I said, "Guinea pigs are also small mammals."

And she said, "I am really sorry, Lucy Rose. But whatever they are they make me feel all wiggly inside and cold outside and I know that is silly but that's just how I feel and I can't help it."

My face went so sad that everyone was quiet and then my mom said, "Do they have any other kind of animal we could watch?"

I was thinking what if I had a tantrum like the girl in the letter? Would I get my way? But just by taking one look I could tell my mom is going to be firm on this one plus I could tell she feels sorry about it. But not as sorry as I feel.

December 7

Today I got a Christmas card from my Michigan friends, Annie and Frannie, and it had their picture on it and I was glad they looked just the same as before. They wrote inside that my dad paid them one dollar EACH to walk his dog that used to be our dog and has the name of Ellie May. I used to walk her for free and I wish I still could but I am a little glad that we left her in Ann Arbor because my dad needs the company, I think. I am bugging my mom for a new dog for here and I told her I would take care of him every minute but she said I have to go to school and she has to go to work and it wouldn't be fair to leave a puppy alone all day. I say no guinea pig and no dog is no fair.

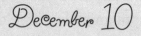 December 10

Since yesterday was Sunday and my mom had off from work we borrowed Madam and Pop's station wagon, which, if you can believe it, is purple, and we went to Frager's Hardware store and bought a Christmas tree that is called Fresh Cut and we went to Grubb's and got a box of candy canes. When we got back to our house I helped my mom put the lights on our tree which took forever on account of they were tangled and then we decorated it.

After dinner, when it was eight-thirty at night which is my exact bedtime and I had already brushed my teeth, my mom let me come downstairs and have cocoa with her in the living room.

She is usually serious like anything about LIGHTS OUT, especially on school nights. But instead we sat on the floor and looked at the Christmas tree and I was glad we had the decorations from before in Ann Arbor but I wondered what my dad was going to put on his tree. Then when I said it my mom pulled one big surprise and let me stay up even longer. We went into the kitchen and we mixed flour and salt and water and food dye to make dough and then I squished some of it through the garlic press and made hair so I could make one ornament with curly black hair that looks like Gumbo and one with red hair that looks like me. When I was done we put them in the oven to make them cook until they got dry and when they did I wrapped them both up in red tissue paper and then I broke off a little piece of our good-smelling Fresh Cut tree and tied it to the front. This morning we sent them by FedEx to my dad in Ann Arbor.

December 12

This afternoon I got an e-mail from my dad and it said: "Dear Lucy Rose, Of all the ornaments I have ever seen, the ones you sent me are my favorites."

And that was a fine feeling for me.

December 15

This morning my mom went to work and had to do a lot of it because she is new and the old people get to pick days off first which my mom says is just fair because when they were new they worked the weekends. For Madam and me this was double A-OK because we had one big plan.

The thing about our new house is that we are short on furniture. My mom says it's no big deal because she likes the house to feel uncluttered which is good feng shui which is how they do houses in China but Madam thinks she is partly saying it to be a good sport and that she would really like a dining room table because, Madam says, "Who wouldn't?"

And I said, "I am one person who agrees with that."

So we went to the tag sale of Madam's friend, Mrs. Greeley, who is 70 and has got a boyfriend who is really an old man friend because he is 72.

They are going to get married and move to San Diego, California, to be closer to Mrs. Greeley's daughter and also to the sun because the boyfriend never wants to shovel another flake of snow in his whole life. Those are fine reasons if you miss your daughter and are against snow, I guess, but I felt like I needed to tell her so I did. "Mrs. Greeley," I said, "moving is not as much fun as you think."

A little bit later, in the back of Mrs. Greeley's house I found an old table with a little bit curvy legs and called out, "Hey, Madam, come look!"

And she did. "It's made of wood from a cherry tree," Madam said. "And I think it's older than me."

"That is one old table," I said, and then I saw a scrape right on the top of it. I told Madam, "Let's find a better one."

"No," Madam said. "This one has good bones."

I think she is wrong about furniture having bones but I don't know everything.

Then the boyfriend showed us four chairs that are also made of cherry tree and Madam wrote a check for all of it.

The man that was in charge of the money box

and is also Mrs. Greeley's great-nephew that goes to college at Georgetown University helped us put the chairs inside the station wagon and tie the table to the top of the car with bungee cords and Mrs. Greeley said, "I am glad they are going to a good home."

And I said, "A very good home."

When we got to my grandparents' house, Pop helped get the table down and put it in the garage, which was really a stable for horses in the olden days. Then we all three put on Pop's old T-shirts and Madam put on jeans which she hardly ever wears, and we worked like crazy to make that table good again.

I helped Pop rub the scrape on the top with sandpaper until it was flat and then Madam gave me big yellow rubber gloves and a fuzzy scratchy blob of stuff that is called steel wool and we rubbed all the old varnish away and when it was smooth we painted the whole table with new shellac which stinks like you wouldn't believe. After that I was so tired I had to lie on the chaise for a while and listen to Pop talk about when he was a boy and had a best friend with the name of Amos whose own mother said he was nothing but trouble and that is one old-time story I like a lot.

December 16

Today I made another e-mail for Madam and it said: "Dear Lucy Rose, What should a person do when they are missing another person?" I signed it "Just Curious" so she would not know it was me.

And I got an e-mail back in about one second and it said: "Dear Curious, I picture them in my head and then I think of all the reasons I love them and then I call them on the phone and tell them."

So I did and when I was done my dad told me all the reasons he loves me, too.

Pretty smart, that Madam.

December 18

This afternoon after school, Madam picked me up and we drove out to the G Street Remnant store and I got to pick out the fabric to cover the chair seats. Even though I really wanted shiny red, I went with my mother's favorite color which is periwinkle blue. I found some with white dots that cost $6 for a yard which Madam said was a deal. When we got home we took off the old cloth which had mean-looking parrots on it and was so gross I didn't even want to touch it. Then Pop stapled the new dotty fabric on and it looks so beautiful that he said, "I can't believe they are the same chairs."

I said, "If Mrs. Greeley saw them she would say the exact same thing."

It is still 7 days until Christmas and I am feeling crazy to tell my mom her present but I am not because telling presents is a little kid thing to do. I am keeping mum, which means quiet and is also a palindrome. But I am going to tell Jonique who is a good one for keeping secrets.

December 20

Today was the last day of school because it's winter break and I brought Mr. Welsh a present of these kind of cheesy cookies that my mom and I made so he wouldn't have to have the sweet kind.

Melonhead gave him a mug, which I know from my dad is one thing that teachers get way too many of. But I didn't say it. That is because I am getting mature, according to Pop.

When I was leaving the classroom Mr. Welsh asked me, "Was December any better than November, Lucy Rose?"

And I told him, "Yes, but I still miss Ann Arbor and my dad and my Michigan grandma and my old house. And my old school. And my friends. And my dog."

He said, "Of course."

Which I appreciated.

And then he said, "Okay, Lucy Rose. For now, I guess I'll hang on to my hat."

Which, I have to say, I still have not laid my eyes on.

December 24

Since it is Christmas Eve we went to Jonique's house which was decorated better than the Mazza Gallerie stores where we went to see Santa Claus. Mrs. McBee wrapped their front door like a giant present with green shiny paper and a big red bow and inside they had a Santa and a Mrs. Claus with brown faces like the McBees and they had angels going up their stairs and a tree with golden balls and silver ribbons and lights that bubble. Mrs. McBee was wearing a Santa hat and a sparkly snowflake sweater and I told her, "You are a beauty, Mrs. McBee!" And she made me the biggest smile.

Then Mr. McBee made cocoa with baby marsh-mallows for everybody and poured it into mugs shaped like Santa heads with handles that are made of Santa's hat. Then Mr. McBee held his mug up in the air and said, "Merry Christmas to all!" and we clanked our mugs together for toasting.

The McBees gave me a reindeer made out of a candy cane with pipe cleaner antlers and googly eyes and I gave Jonique a Friends of the National Zoo pencil with a panda eraser which I told her came from my heart and my mom gave them a jar of pecans that are called roasted because she cooked them herself.

Afterwards we went to Madam and Pop's and put everything under the tree except my mom's present which Madam and Pop and I put under three big blankets on account of wrapping it would take about 50 rolls of paper.

My mom and I are spending the night here at my grandparents' so we could wake up early because I could not stand to wait one extra minute to give my mother the table and chairs even though Madam says I have to stay in bed until 7:30 A.M.

It is the second longest night in my whole life. The first longest was the last night in my old house.

December 25. Christmas

In the morning my mother loved the table so much she danced around and sat in every single chair and said, "This is the best present I've ever gotten."

And then she looked at every chair and said, "The fabric is completely perfect and full of good feng shui."

And my grandmother said I gave her the exactly right thing that she really needed like mad which was safety pins. And my grandfather opened his present which was a lion piggy bank that I got at the tag sale for one dollar which was a lot but worth it because he said it was the handsomest lion in his collection and put it on the fireplace mantel in his office which is the best place he has in the whole house. And I gave Gumbo a tennis ball that I found rolling around on the sidewalk near our house which he loved, I think.

From Santa Claus I got a new red bike with a basket and a bell and a glittery helmet with silver streaks on the side that make you look like you are going really fast. Also he brought me a chef's hat and an apron and a cookbook that is made for kids and a new backpack and socks with toes built in and a jar of macadamia nuts which I love. My aunt Marguerite airmailed me a whole set of pens from Japan where she lives with her husband who works at a bank. They are good for drawing and they make smells when you write. The best one is pink and smells like strawberry cough syrup.

From my aunt Pansy who lives in Atlanta, Georgia, I got a book about flowers which I think is kind of a dopey present but she wrote in the front of it a note that said: "Dear Lucy Rose, Since all the girls in our family are named after flowers you should get to know species." I already know that marguerites are the same as daisies so it's not like I have so much to learn. I am remembering what Madam said about having better luck next year.

And I got a silver necklace with a lighthouse on it from my uncle and aunt who live in Swampscott, Massachusetts. He is named Mike after Pop's father because flower names aren't good for boys and she is named Madelyn but everybody calls her Max. I don't know why. And I also got a painting kit from Madam and Pop. Plus I got a new red writing book that I love and is just from Pop by himself. I told him it was in the nick of time because this old book is almost full on account of all my original thinking.

Later when we were sitting on the new chairs having chocolate croissants and sparkling cider in champagne glasses the door knocker knocked and my mom looked at my grandmother and smiled and the front door opened and my dad walked into the hall! That was the thing that I told the Mazza Gallerie Santa I wanted most of all.

When he saw me my dad bent down on his knees

and made his arms wide and I rushed in and we hugged and hugged and then stopped so he could back up and take a good look at me and he said, "You look prettier than ever, Lucy Rose."

And I said, "You look like a million! And also different."

"New glasses," my dad said.

"Plus your hair is shorter," I said.

"Too short?" he said.

"Nope," I said, "exactly right."

Then my mom said, "Hello, Bob."

And my dad said, "Hello, Lily." And I think they were a little happy to see each other. Then Pop got a chair from the kitchen and my dad sat down with us and ate a croissant and told a funny story about a girl he teaches who didn't know Bingo was a game and just thought it was a name for a dog and then we all started singing "B-I-N-G-O" and it was so fun even though it is a kindergarten song.

In the afternoon my dad and Pop and I went to see the National Christmas Tree which is near the White House and is huge and then we walked around and looked at all fifty trees from all fifty states and Pop took a picture of me and my dad in front of the Michigan tree and then we stood in front of the White House and I waved like mad in case the president was looking out.

At night we all had dinner together. It was craw-fish étouffée which I am not one for eating but is a New Orleans food that Madam loves, so we have it. For dessert we had chocolates from Ann Arbor and a cake that looks like a log but tastes extremely excellent and afterwards I played the song of "The Little Fireflies" on my cello. My dad said, "It really sounds like little fireflies."

And Pop said, "I hope you never learn a song called 'The Little Buffaloes.'"

That was a joke.

Then my dad gave me a little present from my Michigan grandma. Her name is Glamma because when my oldest boy cousin was a baby he couldn't say Grandma and I say that is a good name for her because she is glamorous like anything. Inside the box there was a real gold ring and it fits just right and I have never had a real ring before. Madam says this is not the thing to mention about presents but I bet it cost a lot of money. And I got a Polarfleece pullover from his sister who is my aunt Betsy who has seven kids if you can believe it. I also got a present from my dad which was a red and blue plaid suitcase that has wheels and a handle for pulling. My mom and I ran home and packed it up real fast so I could go stay with my dad at the Capitol Hill Hotel near the train station.

December 28

Of all the things I put in my new suitcase the thing I forgot was my new writing book so I had to wait until now when I am back at home to write about my whole time at the hotel. Before this I never stayed at a hotel actually but when I grow up I plan to stay in a lot of them. For one thing, they have a swimming pool and a whirlpool you can sit in which we did every morning for the whole three days. For another I got my own queen-size bed that was so hugely big that when I lay down in the middle and stretched as hard as I could, I could not touch any of the edges.

On the first day we went to the Full of Beans store and I got a red sweater and orange gloves and some farmer overalls and a jacket that looks like a teenager would wear. After I came out of the dressing room my dad said, "I'm glad I didn't go to the mall in Ann Arbor because you have grown so much, everything I bought would have been too small."

I was surprised because I don't feel like I've grown at all except for my feet.

On the second day I got to invite Jonique over for a swim and lunch at Union train station where she got chicken fingers FINALLY and I got a Hebrew National hot dog with relish and ketchup and we both got chips and Sprites. Jonique asked my dad all about being a teacher and then she asked him, "Do you get to call the principal by her first name?"

And he said, "Yes, but only when there are no kids around."

And Jonique said, "When I am grown I want to be a math teacher first."

"I think you'll be a fine math teacher," my dad told her.

"And then I would like to be a principal," Jonique said.

And my dad said, "I would too," which was something I never knew before.

Then Jonique said, "If you are ever a principal and I am a teacher, can I call you by your first name?"

He said, "Yes, but only when there are no kids around."

She said, "It's a deal."

And I said, "If you get to be a principal don't make the just-starting teachers feel nervous, okay?"

And he said that was a deal too.

On the last day my dad and I had room service muffins and they came with the tiniest jar of strawberry jam that is the cutest thing in America. I saved it for my mom for a present. Then, while we were eating, I asked my dad, "Can you move to Washington and can we go back to being unseparated?"

But he said, "I'm sorry because I know you would like that, but no. Your mom and I talked it over a lot, Lucy Rose, and this is what we need to do."

I am sorry too but that is what I had the feeling he would say. He also said he loves me and misses me and that my mom is one good mother and I said, "I am one person who agrees with that."

And he said, "I'll come see you on Presidents' Day weekend for sure."

And I told my dad, "You are one good pal and one good pal-indrome."

Then I told him that came from original thinking.

And he agreed.

JANUARY

If I was the writer of "Dear Lucy Rose" this would be my best recommendation for kids: Do NOT eat licorice before breakfast, especially if you have the kind of mother that is firm about breakfast and not wild for sugar, and I do have that kind exactly.

Here is why I know this is good advice: Back at Halloween I made a deal with myself that I would eat one piece of candy every morning. I also made a deal that I would not tell my mom because it is for sure that she would not approve. So, I have been keeping all my candy under my bed in a party shoe box from the Payless store which is a secret from everybody except Jonique. Every morning after I brush my teeth I eat one piece, usually while I put on my socks and if it is chewy it lasts until I tie on my cowgirl bandana if I am wearing it which I usually am. In November I ate the Twix bars and the Skittles and the peanut M&M's. And in December I ate the plain M&M's and the Snickers and Reese's Peanut Butter Cups

72

plus the chocolate Santa that was in my stocking.

So now that winter break is over the only things left are the not-so-hot ones like Goldeberg's Peanut Chews and stretchy orange circus peanuts which I actually hate and one teensy box of hard raisins and some stuck-together black licorice. And since I am going from best to worst and I like licorice better than raisins, I ate it. Actually I ate all the pieces because since they were stuck they only count as one. And when I got downstairs my mom said, "Lucy Rose, what is the matter with your teeth?"

And I said, "Nothing."

But she said, "Did you eat something?"

So I said, "No," and kept my lips down so she couldn't look. And then I sat down at the new table for a V8 juice which I love but this is the thing I never knew before: When your mouth tastes like black licorice and then you drink V8, it turns into the worst flavor you could ever think of. I mean the absolutely, extremely worst. And I couldn't spit it out. And that was the very minute I started to learn the hardest lesson.

We were having a rushing morning because we were late like anything which is rather usual for us.

My mom was putting cream cheese on a bagel so I could eat it on the walk to school, and right then she said, "Shake a leg, Lucy Rose. Drink your juice so we can hit the road."

I did not want to tell her about the lie so I swallowed it up and it tasted so bad it made me feel woozy in the stomach and in the head. I was still trying not to talk on account of not wanting to show my teeth but nodding my head to say yes made it feel even spinnier. And then we had to rush into our coats and I smooshed my feet into my cowgirl boots and we got going but I felt terrible like you could not believe. We walked down Fourth Street, past Mrs. Greeley's house which has a SOLD sign in the front yard and past an old, used-up Christmas tree someone put out for the trash and then we turned on Madam and Pop's street which is Constitution Avenue and my mom kept saying we should step on it and I should eat my bagel. And thinking about the cream cheese made my stomach feel even sicker. Then I saw Nada from grade 6 walking ahead of us and Melonhead and his mother were just across the street waiting for the light to change

and all of a sudden I threw up and it got in the grass and on my cowgirl boots and a little on my new jacket.

My mom said, "Eye-yi-yi," which is what she says when she's got stress and this was an extremely lot of stress for her and for me because I could see that Nada turned around and was looking and I could hear Melonhead's mother tell him, "That is not funny, Adam."

And I could hear him say, "Yes it is."

And my mom was what Madam calls beside herself. "I can't believe I didn't realize you were sick!" she told me in her soupy-sad voice. "I'm so sorry, Lucy Rose."

She kneeled down on the sidewalk and wiped my face with old Kleenex from her pocket and gave me a hug. Then she whooshed me off to my grandparents' because she had to get to work because of *News at Noon* needing art and when we got inside I heard her say to Madam, "I just feel rotten leaving her when she's got the flu."

When she said that I felt even worse.

At my grandparents' I got a big fuss made over me for being sick. Madam rushed around and got me ginger ale which she only allows in the case of parties or emergencies and she put my school clothes and my jacket in the washing machine and gave me her softy slippers and Pop's Penn State University T-shirt to wear. She took my temperature and, even though I didn't have one, propped me up in bed with a lot of pillows in case I felt weak. Pop brought the little TV into my room which is something Madam recommends against in "Dear Lucy Rose" but she made an exception because she said I was so sick with a virus. By then I felt good in my stomach but bad in my heart and was wishing I did have a virus instead.

There was not much on TV except *Oprah* and I am not one for that show especially when there are crying ladies on it. So instead I was lying flat looking at the ceiling at a little crack that looks like a piece of broccoli when Pop came into my room with the Chinese checkers which is what he plays because he hates Parcheesi. I got the red marbles and he got yellow and we jumped around and Pop didn't say too much and then after a while I said, "I have a truth to tell you, Pop."

And he said, "You do?"

And I said, "Yes. It is the truth about a big lie."

And Pop said, "A really big one?"

Then he listened about the licorice and how my mom asked me if I ate something and that I said "No." And I said about the V8 and even telling it made me feel sick all over again. Then I told him how I felt bad about getting free ginger ale and TV from Madam and even worse about making everybody, especially my mom, think I had a virus. And then I started to cry.

Pop gave me a big hug and patted my hair for a while and then he said, "The thing about lies is that big or little, they make you feel bad but they usually don't make you throw up."

"I wish I never said it," I told him.

And he said, "That is usually the feeling good people get after they tell a lie."

So I said, "What do I do?"

"Well," he said, "the only way to fix a lie is to tell the truth and that's called being honorable."

So at 6:00 I went downstairs and sat on the steps and was nervous and waited for my mom. The minute she came in I ran up to her and made a big confession.

She said, "Thank you for telling me the truth, Lucy Rose."

I said, "It's because I'm honorable."

"I'm glad you weren't really sick," my mom said. And then she sat on the steps and I sat on her lap and after a while she said, "What do you think your punishment should be, Lucy Rose?"

I hated to say it. "No TV for the longest time," I said. "And no candy."

"Those are two ideas," she said.

And then she was quiet and after a few minutes she said, "Throwing up in front of Adam Melon is probably punishment enough."

January 9

When I came home from school today I told my mom, "That is one thing you were right about."

"I was?" she said.

"Every time I got near Melonhead he would make throw-up noises and hold his nose and he would not stop talking about it until Mr. Welsh asked him if he would like to go stand in the hall until he could find his manners."

"That's annoying," my mom said.

"It gets worse," I told her. "When we were on the

playground and Mr. Welsh was not, Melonhead started singing a song he made up called 'Hold Your Nose, It's Lucy Rose' which made me wild with anger."

"I don't blame you," she said.

"But then Jonique told him, 'Adam, If you don't quit it I will tell everyone about the time you stepped in dog poop.' And he said he didn't care but I think he did because he stopped singing. And then later when I was waiting for Madam to pick me up and he was waiting for his mom and we were the last two from third grade I told him that he should think of other people's feelings, especially mine, and he said something that I could not hear very well but it sounded kind of like 'Sorry.'"

"That sounds like a wretched day," my mom said.

"It was," I told her. "Wretched like you can't believe."

January 14

I talked to my dad on the phone like I do every weekend and I told him about the whole thing. He said that one time he ate bad ham salad and threw up in front of his whole 5th grade class so he knows my pain. And he said that ever since then he has not been one for eating ham salad and I said I thought that after this I would not be one for eating black licorice. And he said, "Well, Lucy Rose, everyone has to learn about not lying so it's good to learn it early."

"Did you learn early?" I asked him.

"Yep," he said. "When I was 8 years old I was mad at my sister so I hid her shoes so she'd be late for school and when Glamma found them in the laundry basket I told her I didn't do it."

So I said, "What happened?"

And he said, "When my sister had to stay after school I felt bad and confessed and Glamma made me tell her teacher what I did."

Even though it happened a long time ago, my dad's story made me feel pretty much better. And it made me feel like he was not so far away.

January 20

All day I was still thinking about everything that happened and I wrote an e-mail that said: "Dear

Lucy Rose, I would like to make you a recommendation and that is that you tell kids not to lie. Signed, A Person Against Lying."

January 21

When I got home from school there was an e-mail and it said: "Dear Person Against Lying, Good idea. I will."

FEBRUARY

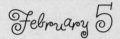

February 5

We have an all-valentine rule which Mr. Welsh is extremely serious about. The rule is that everyone has to bring a valentine for everyone else otherwise it isn't fair which is a plan I would be on the side of except it means I have to give one to Melonhead, which I do not feel like doing even if he did say "Sorry" which he might not have.

Today I got to go to Jonique's after school and Mrs. McBee gave us valentine's milk which was really strawberry Quik and Jonique said, "When you do your valentines I think you should be allowed to skip Melonhead."

And I said, "I am one girl who agrees with that idea."

February 6

Today at recess I waited by the door to ask Mr. Welsh for an exception to the valentine rule. And the first thing he said was, "Why?"

And I said, "What if I only have 22 cards and we have 23 people?"

And he said, "If that happens you should make the last one by hand."

"What if I forget someone?" I asked him.

"You won't," Mr. Welsh said. "You have a terrific memory, Lucy Rose."

Plus, I thought, that would actually be a lie.

"What if I don't want to give every single person a card?" I asked him.

"Your other choice is to give nobody a card," he said. "But I don't think that is much of a solution, do you?"

So now I have to find a card for Melonhead.

February 13

Pop has sympathy for the valentine problem so he took me to Grubb's where I tried to find one box with 22 good cards and one bad card. But it turned out they don't come that way and even the good cards were P-U. So we bought a pocket box of conversation heart candies and some Elmer's glue and Eddie gave us some doilies that he has in the back room where he keeps the Evening in Paris dusting powder and other things that take up valuable shelf space and nobody wants to buy.

When we got back to Madam and Pop's house I dumped all the candy hearts on the kitchen table. I saved HOT STUFF for Madam and COOL DUDE for Pop and LUV YOU for my dad and PRETTY LADY for my mom. Then I started making little piles. I put U R A QT and SWEET GIRL and FOR KEEPS in Jonique's pile. I gave Pierra one that said IN STYLE because she is. I saved COOL GUY for Sam and AWESOME for Emily Kate and DREAMY for Robinson, GAL PAL for Kathleen and ROCK STAR for John Gallagher who is our new lunch aide and can play the guitar. After I got done with everybody except Melonhead I looked at what I had left which was bad news for me. I ate TRUE LOVE just to be sure I didn't accidentally glue it to his doily. Also MARRY ME which was even worse. What was left after that was U R KIND, TRÈS CHIC, CALL ME, and ROMEO. Pop ate CALL ME because he said, "I certainly don't want Melonhead tying up our phone line."

And then he ate TRÈS CHIC which is a French way to say fashionable which Madam said wasn't really appropriate for a boy but I was considering anyway. Then Pop went off to feed Gumbo and I got the greatest idea in my life which was to lick, carefully, all the letters off of ROMEO which worked great and turned it into a plain purple heart. Then I glued the hearts onto the doilies and wrote "From Lucy Rose" with a glitter pen on the bottom and put them in the envelopes that Madam uses to pay her bills and then I put them in the extremely très chic pink and red covered shoe box my mom made for me. At dinner I told how I solved my number one valentine problem and Madam said she was surprised at me but it didn't sound like in a good way.

I went to bed on time but I could not sleep from feeling bad which made me surprised and I got up and took out Melonhead's card and opened it up and picked off the spit heart and pasted on U R KIND which was more than I wanted to say but was all I had left and put it back in the box for the morning.

After I gave my card to Melonhead he gave me a card back. It said YOU ARE A FART.

This is the question I e-mailed to Madam today: "Dear Lucy Rose, Do you know a good way to get even with somebody? Signed, One Steaming Mad Person."

The answer came. It said: "Dear Steaming Mad, I know lots of ways to get even but it's better to get over it. Try."

I say P-U on that advice.

I got up at 6:00 this morning because of excitement over my dad coming for Presidents' Day

weekend even though his airplane was not landing until 10:30. So I sat on the front porch with my suitcase that could hardly close because I had so many things inside of it, and waited. After a while my mom brought me cinnamon toast and sat with me until he came in a taxi and picked me up. When we got to the hotel he gave me a tiny box that is shaped like a heart and has four pieces of chocolate that is from him and pink nail polish from Glamma, who is one for wearing polish. Also makeup and stick-on eyelashes and sometimes fake nails. I am not allowed to wear fake nails but when I go to her house she lets me try on her lipstick and she paints my real nails any color I pick which is a hard job because Glamma has more than thirty bottles. My best ones are Cocoa-Cabana and Moonlight Delight and Coral Gables. Glamma has hair that is called Strawberry Blond and she dresses like a movie star and she has a golden purse that I love like anything. One time I told Madam that she should dress like Glamma but she said every lady has to pick her own style.

At the hotel my dad and I went swimming because now that is one of our main hotel activities that we do together. On Saturday we took the Metro and I told my dad, "This subway is one thing that makes Washington, D.C., a good place for living."

I knew he would agree with that but I like to point out the good things just in case knowing them might make him want to move here someday. We rode the Red Line to the Dolls' House Museum. The best thing I saw was a cake that was as small as a penny. It wasn't real.

On the way home we got off at the Mall which is not the shopping kind of mall but a big park near the Washington Monument. There is a merry-go-round and I got to ride on it and my dad took my picture on a pink horse and when I got off the ticket-taking man used my dad's camera and took a picture of both of us together and I made my movie star smile that shows almost all my teeth at once and the ticket guy said to my dad, "She's the spitting image of you," which I thought was rude because I am no spitter.

But my dad said, "That means you look like me."

"Except for the mustache," the man said.

So that was a pleasing thing after all.

On Saturday night my dad helped me polish my toenails which is something that he is really not very good at but I acted like he is. Then I had to sit still and wait for them to get dry. I told my dad about the valentines and he said he did not know what to do with a boy like Melonhead.

So I asked him, "But what if he went to your school? What would you do then?"

"Probably have a lot of parent-teacher conferences," my dad said.

MARCH

Lately when things that are good happen I have been shouting "Yippee-yi-yo, cowgirl!" Which is exactly what I did yell this morning because our tables got moved again. This is actually a double good thing because now Melonhead is sitting up front where the talkers go and I am over by Jake. I'm so close that when Mr. Welsh is not paying good attention to me, I can poke my finger through the cage and try to get Jake to lick it. And even though Jonique is not at my table she is at the next one so she is pretty near me and also Jake. The other kids at my table are Amir who is an ESL kid, that means English as a Second Language which it is for him because he comes from overseas and is just learning about how we talk in America. Also there is Marian who is nice. She is a nail biter. I think it's because she is nervous. And right across from me is Kathleen and that is a handy thing because she told me that Jake's favorite food is Cheerios. So I made a whole Baggie full and took them to school and put them in my desk so if Jake is looking hungry, which he does a lot of the time, I can drop one in his cage. I know he appreciates this because every time I do it he snarfs it right up.

March 12

I was telling about Jake and the Cheerios today when we were taking a family walk and I was wishing I could figure out a way to get my mom to like small mammals when Pop said, "Maybe, if it is all right with Mr. Welsh, Jake can spend spring break at our house."

"That makes good sense," Madam said to my mom. "Lucy Rose is going to be with us when you're at work and when she's at home she can just walk over and feed him and change the shavings."

"That is an inspired plan," my mom said.

"And," Madam said, "it will be nice for Gumbo to have another animal in the house even if it is just temporary."

Then Pop said, "Madam will make little guinea pig clothes for him."

And I said, "Great plan!" because it is.

But Madam said Pop was just joking about the clothes.

And then I said, "Wait one minute, everybody. I still have to get Mr. Welsh to pick me. And so far that has been one big flop." Madam looked like she was thinking up some advice but I told her not to try. "This is one problem that even an expert grandmother can't fix," I said.

But Madam is not one to give up so she said her recommendation anyway. "Lucy Rose, sometimes you have to let someone know you are serious and not just jumping on an idea."

"How?" I asked her.

"Sometimes when I have something serious to say I write the person a letter," Madam explained. "Not e-mail or a note. A real letter."

So I took that recommendation and when we got back I got a felt-tip pen from my grandfather's study and some of Madam's letter paper that has the name of Lucy Rose on the top which is one handy thing about having the same name and I sat down at Madam's extremely huge working desk and here is what I wrote:

Dear Mr. Welsh,

I know a lot of kids want to keep Jake for the holidays but probably not as much as me. I have an extremely lot of experience with dogs because I used to have one in Ann Arbor and my grandparents still do have one named Gumbo. I walk her a lot and take her to Grubb's and never leave her tied to the fence while I am inside and then forget and go back home without her which the rest of the family does sometimes, so it is for sure that I am the most responsible. Also, I would feed Jake and make sure he didn't get wet which I know can do in a guinea pig. And I would give Jake love and I promise to keep him safe. Also I have six dollars and forty cents that is mine for helping my grandmother get her office organized which means I can buy his food. So I would really like it if you would pick me. Please.

Sincerely from your student,

Lucy Rose

March 13

So, the very first thing today I gave Mr. Welsh the letter and he read it while I stood right there watching.

"Lucy Rose," he said, "you make a good case for yourself. You may be Jake's keeper for the second half of spring break."

I looked at him hard. "Is this for serious?" I asked him.

"Yep," Mr. Welsh said. "Your letter convinced me."

"Yippee-yi-yo, cowgirl! Thank you, thank you, Mr. Welsh," I said and I gave him one big hug.

Then he said, "Adam Melon is going to keep him for the first five days, so you two can figure out how to make the trade."

I was so happy about my days that I tried not to think about his. At recess Jonique and I sat in the mulch under the jungle gym bridge in the kindergarten playground and ate her Fruit Roll-Up and I told her she could help with taking care of Jake. She said, "You are one great person for sharing, Lucy Rose."

I did not say it out loud but I think she is right about that.

Since my mom had to work a weekend day she had this day off and she picked me up from school and I told her and we both ran the whole way to

Madam and Pop's house so they could know too. When I got there I hugged Madam so hard because it was her advice on writing the letter that made Mr. Welsh pick me. When Pop heard the news he told Madam, "You better get busy making those guinea pig costumes." And that had us laughing our heads off.

And then my mom said this was such a great day that she was going to make my two best foods which are lasagna and blueberry cobbler for a celebrating dinner.

After dessert I made an e-mail for my dad and I told him all about everything and he made an e-mail back that said: "Congratulations! I am proud of you. That was an excellent letter you wrote to Mr. Welsh."

And I wrote back the words: "One thing about me lately is that I am getting mature like you can't believe."

March 17

Today at recess Jonique said to me, "Can I come to Madam and Pop's with you after school?"

But I said, "Nope, because one thing I have learned is that if it's a holiday, your house is better."

So when school was over we went to Jonique's and Mrs. McBee was waiting for us with shamrock cookies that came from the Sweetheart Bakery, and man-o-man, were they dee-lish. And she gave me and Jonique stickers that say KISS ME, I'M IRISH! And then she did.

I told her that actually I really am half Irish because my dad is and that's why he has red hair and so do I. So Mrs. McBee said, "Then I'd better kiss you again for luck!" And she did, again, right on the top of my head.

And I said to her, "You are the queen of all the McBees!"

March 27

My mom and I went to the pet store and my mom bought a bag of guinea pig food and with my own money I bought a blue plastic ball with a bell inside for Jake to play with and when we got home I got out my painting kit and painted a big sign that has palm trees and hearts and smile faces on it and says WELCOME JAKE so that when he gets here he will know he is in guinea pig paradise.

APRIL

April 1

I am waiting so hard for my turn with Jake that I can hardly keep my brain on anything else even April Fools' Day which is one of my favorite holidays. But I still did a trick on my mom this morning by turning the clock radio to 9:13 to make her think we were late for school. I waited until she was all the way dressed and giving me a Luna bar for an emergency fast breakfast and had us out the door on the porch and then I screamed, "April Fools'!" at the top of my lungs and laughed so hard I almost fell over.

At lunchtime Jonique took a bite out of her bologna sandwich and there was a big black plastic spider inside. I think Mrs. McBee saved it from Halloween. When I say she is a genius, it is no joke. All day long Melonhead kept saying, "Hi, Lucy Rose," and giving me pats on the back. Only it was not to be friendly. It was to put Post-it notes on my sweater that said, "Please pinch me!"

Luckily, Jonique told me and we got the big idea

of putting one of those notes upside down on Melonhead's chair and he sat on it so he had "Please pinch me!" on his butt for a lot of the afternoon which made Jonique and me laugh our heads off but the bad thing is no one pinched him.

Then when I got home from school Pop pretended he had a bean stuck in his nose. I fell for it and so did Madam and while Pop was jumping around holding his nostril she kept saying, "How does a sixty-two-year-old man get a bean stuck in his nose?"

Then Pop got a Kleenex and blew his nose and then he said, "Why, that's not a bean, it's a clementine." And it was. He is the best joker in the family.

April 8

Here is a good thing: Since today was teacher planning day we did not have school. And since it was a workday for my mom and Madam and Pop had to go be volunteers at the Friendship House day care nursery, I got to stay at Jonique's house for almost the whole day which was excellent because they have Cartoon Network which my mother thinks is not worth the money. And we had Bagel Bites for lunch and Sprite, if you can believe it. And Mr. McBee came home from work at 5:30 and had us laughing with his jokes which are all about elephants. But even with all of those many good things the only thing on my brain is how many days until Jake will be at my house. 9 days, that's how many.

April 12

Finally it is the day we get out of school for Easter and Passover break and at 3:00 Mr. Welsh told me and Melonhead to stay after. Then he showed us how to load up the water bottle which I already knew. And then he said, "Fresh H_2O every day."

I happen to know that H_2O means water. "Right-O, H_2O," I said.

"Of course," Adam Melon said.

And then Mr. Welsh said, "Only one handful of food at a time."

And we both said "Okay" to that.

"Can you clean the cage every day?" he asked us.

"I can," I said.

I wanted to say, "But I would not be counting on Melonhead." But I didn't on account of having maturity.

At 4:00 Melonhead's dad came to school and loaded Jake and his enormous cage into the back of the Melons' minivan and told me that they would bring him to my grandparents' house in five days.

April 14. Easter Sunday

Waiting for Jake feels long but the days are going a little fast because of Easter which is today.

Madam is wild for Easter and she and my mom spent all afternoon yesterday making big baskets of pansies and tiny daffodils and hyacinths which look pretty but to tell the truth, which is something I am surely trying to do these days, not as pretty as the McBees'. Mrs. McBee hung plastic eggs all over the tree in their front yard and she has a sign that says BUNNY CROSSING and another one that says THE EASTER BUNNY STOPS HERE. This morning Jonique and I both got baskets full of chocolate bunnies and colored eggs and jelly beans. Jonique wore a dress made of the orangey color of apricot insides and a white hat with striped ribbon for going to the Faith Tabernacle church and I wore a yellow skirt with a light blue sweater set and a pink hairband for going to St. Joseph's and while I was there I saw a palindrome which was a nun. After church the McBees came to Madam and Pop's to eat hot cross buns which look better than they taste, even though Mrs. McBee said to Madam, "These are delicious."

And I was surprised because I didn't think Mrs. McBee would say a lie but she did, over and over so then I thought maybe she actually does like them. When we were away from the grown-ups, Jonique said the truth: "These are P-U."

April 17

Finally it's the day I have been waiting for all year and Melonhead and his mom came over to Madam and Pop's at 11:00 sharp. Pop and Mrs. Melon carried Jake's cage inside and we put it in the morning room with newspaper underneath and then Melonhead said, "Guess what?"

And I said "What?"

And he said, "I taught Jake some tricks."

"Like what?" I asked him.

"Like this," he said, and he took Jake out of the cage and put him on his shoulder and put Cheerios in his hair and Jake climbed up and ate the Cheerios.

I could hardly stand it especially since I'm the one who has been giving Jake Cheerios all this time. Plus I think Melonhead is a big bragger. So I was glad like anything when those Melons left and the first thing I did was call Jonique on the phone and she came running over triple-fast to help me set up the guinea pig paradise.

The first thing we did was dump out the Melon water and put fresh water from our house in the bottle. We also put in new food and we stuck our arms in the cage and gave Jake a lot of petting and showed him his new ball with the bell which he didn't act interested in even when we pushed it around so it would make noise. He just sat there looking wiggy. I thought we should take him out but Pop said we should not especially because it might make Gumbo go berserk.

We stayed right by the cage all afternoon and

only took one break which was to walk to Grubb's because Madam needed thumbtacks. Mostly we sat in front of the cage and ate our lunch which was sandwiches of peanut butter and guava paste which let me tell you is not at all as good as grape jelly but Madam thinks it is a good experience for a person to eat things from other countries which guava paste is, so she doesn't even buy normal jelly. Jonique was a good sport about it and I was thinking that maybe Jake would like a little sandwich piece but when I called my mom at work she said it wouldn't be a good idea so we gave him more Cheerios and mostly we just sat.

April 18

This morning my mom and I went out to breakfast at Jimmy T's Place on East Capitol Street and I had chocolate chip pancakes and she had a cheese omelet and we split a little plate of bacon and on the way back we stopped by to get Jonique and then we went to Madam and Pop's for guinea pig watching and my mom went to the farmers' market to buy sourdough bread.

Jake was sitting in the corner of his cage looking a little sad so I played my cello for him and Jonique did the song of "America the Beautiful" and then we both sang "Seventy-six Trombones" which we learned from watching *The Music Man* on TV. I have to say, Jake did not look like he was liking it too much.

Then I got to thinking about Melonhead and his tricks and it just made me wild inside and I was thinking that I can teach Jake better tricks and then Jonique and I had a conference and I said, "We HAVE to get him out of the cage, otherwise we can't teach him."

And she said, "Are you sure, Lucy Rose?"

And I said, "Sure, I'm sure."

And she said, "Okay."

So we got him out of that cage and we started by doing Melonhead's trick. Jake went right for it and you can't believe how funny it feels to have a guinea pig walking on your head.

And then Jonique said, "We should put him back, I think."

But I said, "I think we should not."

Jonique looked like she was not going to be

agreeing with that but then she said, "All right, I guess."

So I made a line of Cheerios on the floor and she carried Jake over by the coffee table and I said, "Eat!" and pointed to the Cheerios and Jake did but it wasn't really much of a trick so I put him on the coffee table which is glass and then I climbed under it and pretended I was tickling him on his stomach which made Jonique snort with laughing and then at that minute the worst thing happened. Gumbo came into the room and started barking like a maniac which must have made Jake feel skittery because he jumped off the table and onto the sofa and onto the floor and went tearing down the hall and Gumbo was running after him and I had to grab Gumbo by his legs and I yelled at Jonique to catch Jake and she went running after him and Gumbo started barking his poodle head off. Then Jonique was calling for me saying, "Jake is nowhere!"

Gumbo was wiggling like crazy, trying to run down the hall, so I yelled. "He has to be SOME-PLACE! Are you looking everywhere?"

And she hollered, "I can't tell if he went into

Pop's office or the other way into the dining room or straight ahead into the back hall or maybe into the kitchen."

Then I got nervous like anything and Jonique said, "We should get Pop."

But I didn't want to on account of he had already given us the warning that this could happen so I said, "Come on, Jonique. Let's find him ourselves real fast."

Just then Jonique yelled, "There he goes!" and Gumbo made a big break away from me and started jumping all over the hall making sniffing noises and Jonique and I went chasing into Pop's office but we were too late and Jake was gone again. I got scared right then.

Right at that second Madam came up from her picture frame room and Pop came downstairs from where he was lying on the chaise doing his best thing which is the *New York Times* crossword puzzle. And Madam said, "What's the matter, girls?"

Jonique said, "We are in a disaster."

And I said about Jake getting out.

And Pop said, "Jake got out?"

And I said, "Yes."

"By himself?" Pop asked me.

"Not exactly," I said. "We took him out."

"So he could do tricks," Jonique told Pop.

"Okay," Pop said. "Don't panic."

He didn't say one thing about what he already said not to do which I appreciated.

Madam just said, "Think, everyone. If you were a guinea pig where would you hide?"

"I don't know," I said and I started to cry.

And Pop said, "Lucy Rose, we are a family of problem solvers and this is just another problem we will solve."

That helped me to stop crying but I told him, "I am really feeling stress."

Jonique had the good idea to put Cheerios in the hall so we did. And then I called my mom who was at our house painting the laundry room and she came and even though she is against small mammals she made herself brave and helped us look. And look. And look. Me and Mom and Madam and Pop and Jonique. And we did not find him. The later it was getting the more nervous I was feeling. We were trying everything including we took off our shoes so our clomping wouldn't scare him. When it got to be night Madam made chicken noodle soup for dinner but Jonique and I did not want to stop and eat, so Madam poured it into mugs so we could all drink while we looked, even the grown-ups. We made a big inspection of Madam and Pop's room and my room and Madam's office and the bathroom and the closets and we did not see him. Then I realized that the problem was that while we were moving, Jake was probably moving too and I didn't know if we would ever find him. "I wish I had listened to you, Pop," I said.

"Me too," Jonique told Pop.

"Some temptations are hard to resist, girls," Pop said.

"This was one of those," I said.

Finally at 10:30 my mom said we had to go to bed and that we would start fresh in the morning. So Jonique and I got under the estate sale quilt and I told her the truth. "This is my worst mistake ever."

"Mine too," Jonique said.

"Worse than the licorice," I told her.

"Worse than the time I said that really bad word," she said.

"What word?" I asked her.

"That would be saying it twice," Jonique said.

"What if I have to tell Mr. Welsh?" I asked her. "I promised I would keep Jake safe."

"That is a hard thing to think about," Jonique said.

"What if Jake doesn't know where he is and gets scared?" I said. "What if we never get him back?"

"The only single thing I can think of to say is that I will help you every minute until we find him," Jonique said.

I told Jonique that she is what my mom calls a tough-times friend and that is somebody who sticks with you always, even when something bad that happens is actually your fault.

And Jonique said, "Of course I am, Lucy Rose. You are my best friend."

Even though I felt misery inside I also felt a little good from hearing that.

April 19

When I woke up this morning I had a plan. I went down to the kitchen with Jonique and I told Madam and Pop and my mom, "Everybody, I have a serious thing to say."

"Let's hear it," Pop said.

So I told them, "I know what I have to do."

And everybody waited and I said, "I have to call Adam Melon. And I have to ask him to come over and help."

Jonique made a breath-sucking sound. And Madam made her wise eyes. And my mom nodded her head.

"Problem solving is rarely easy," Pop said.

Then I did call and I told Mrs. Melon about the emergency and she said she would bring Adam right over. She did and I was thinking that Melonhead was going to be mean about it but he was actually nice.

"The next class of Mr. Welsh's should give Jake the name of Harry Houdini after that old-time magician who could escape from everything," he said.

That made me feel better because it made it sound like we would find Jake. And then Melonhead said, "I have practice capturing guinea pigs because last week when I was in charge, Jake got away from me."

"This is the greatest news," I said. "How did you get him back?"

"It was easier to capture him because before I took him out of the cage I shut the door to the room," Melonhead told me.

"I wish I had thought about doing that," I said.

It was Melonhead's idea that Jake would probably look for a hiding place and we should start in the basement and work our way up to the top floor. "This is a search-and-rescue mission," he told Madam. "We will need a flashlight."

Madam gave him the one she keeps for if the electricity goes out and then he put guinea pig food in his pockets and Melonhead and Jonique and I went downstairs and we climbed all around the picture frame room and flashed the flashlight at all of the frames and looked hard but we did not find any clues at all. "One thing to look for is poop," Melonhead said. "Jake will probably poop wherever he goes. Guinea pigs are like that."

Jonique said, "Yuck."

But I said, "I would be happy for any clue, even if it's poop."

And then we went in the furnace room which is the scariest room in the house and we saw nothing. And Melonhead said we had to be very quiet and listen for scritching noises so we all held our breath and waited but we didn't hear one single scritch. But then we did hear my mom and Madam calling and we went up and Madam said, "The Cheerios are missing and I am pretty sure Gumbo didn't eat them."

"I think Jake ate them," my mom said. "And then crawled through this hole in the floor where the radiator pipes go through."

"So where is he?" I asked.

And my mom said, "I think he has gotten underneath the floorboards."

Then I felt sick with worry that we would never find him.

But all of a sudden Jonique said, "I have a very great idea! Follow me!"

She ran back to the basement and into the olden-days kitchen and Melonhead ran after her and so did I. "One of us should get in the dumbwaiter," Jonique said. "Then they can ride up and look through the slot on the side to find him or at least leave him some food."

Melonhead said, "I'll do it!"

But I said, "No. I lost him so I should do it."

And I didn't say I was scared to pieces which I was.

But then Melonhead said, "Lucy Rose, if you let me do it I will trade you my good lunches for your bad lunches for the rest of the year."

I couldn't believe it. "You don't have to give me your good lunches," I said. "You can do it if you want."

"Thanks!" Melonhead said.

Then I was a little embarrassed feeling. "Besides," I said, "it'll take me and Jonique to pull the rope that makes the dumbwaiter box go up because it's not electric or anything."

So Melonhead smooshed himself into the dumbwaiter and there was hardly any room left and then he said, "Raise her up!"

Jonique and I yanked on the rope with all of our muscles and the dumbwaiter went up and Melonhead went with it and we pulled and pulled until we could only see an empty space, like if you saw elevator insides without seeing the elevator, only smaller. Then we pulled even harder and our arms felt like they were coming out of their sockets and we held on but then I screamed, "Watch out!" because I couldn't hold on another second and neither could Jonique and the rope just got away and I didn't breathe at all waiting for the crash.

But nothing happened.

We called up, "Are you okay?"

And he yelled back, "Yes."

"Look through the slot," Jonique told him. "What do you see?"

"I can see the space between the basement ceiling and the upstairs floor," Melonhead said.

"I mean do you see Jake?" I shouted up to him.

"Nope," he said. "But I'll put some food in the in-between place and then after I get down we'll send it back up and maybe Jake will find it and walk through the slot and be captured in the dumbwaiter!"

I was depressed with that news.

"Let her down," Melonhead said.

So we pulled the rope but nothing happened. Then we swung on it and nothing happened. Then Melonhead said, "Hurry up, Lucy Rose. It's hot in here."

And I said, "It's stuck."

Then Melonhead went quiet and I went frantic because now Jake and Melonhead were both stuck in the walls and I said, "I'll get Pop."

"Oh, brother!" Jonique said, shaking her head so her braids flew side to side. "He'll probably be mad at us."

And I said, "Probably, but we can't just leave Melonhead in there forever."

And she said she was one who agreed with that because after a while he would be starving, so we ran for Pop and he and Madam and my mom came to the basement and started calling up things to Melonhead. "Help is here," Pop yelled and he pulled on the rope.

"Don't worry," Madam said, even though Pop was not having luck getting him down.

But my mother looked at me and looked at Jonique with mad eyes and she said, "Whatever made you girls think this was a good idea?"

Jonique looked like she was about to cry.

"Well," Pop said, "you have to give them credit for original thinking and a certain amount of nerve."

"But poor Adam Melon," my mom said.

"Adam Melon is probably having the time of his life," Pop said.

And then we all went up to the kitchen where

the dumbwaiter goes up to. The problem is that the door to it has been screwed shut since they remade the kitchen so Pop got a crows bar and a screwdriver and a hammer and he and my mom started to try to unwind the screws to open the door and Pop called out, "How is it down there?" in his echoing voice.

And Melonhead yelled back, "It's small."

"I'll bet," Pop said.

Then Melonhead shouted back, "I guess you really had to be a dumb waiter to ride in this thing."

Pop didn't tell him that before now only food rode in it because it might make him frantic to realize he was the first human to do it.

Madam and Jonique and I went back to the basement in case the dumbwaiter got unstuck and came back down again. Then someone would be waiting for Melonhead when he got out. After a while we could hear Pop yelling down, "Only one screw left to go!"

And then Adam Melon started yelling at the top of his lungs, "I see him!"

For just one second I forgot who him was and

then Melonhead shouted, "I am shining my flashlight right on him!"

"You are?" Jonique shouted. "For real?"

"Yep. Jake is just sitting in the in-between looking at me," Melonhead yelled.

I was hardly breathing from my nerves. "Is he near or far?" I hollered.

"Near. I'm putting my arm through the slot. I'm touching fur!"

Then I was hardly breathing from happiness.

We could hear him say, "Come here, Jake."

And then he said, "No! No! Wrong way."

"Which wrong way?" Jonique screamed.

"He's going up through the floor where a pipe is," Melonhead said.

Jonique and I and Madam ran back up from the basement to the hall by the back staircase where we could hear scritching in the wall and it was getting higher and my mom came out from the kitchen and said, "It sounds like Jake is climbing up the pipes to the upstairs bathroom."

So we all except for Pop ran up there and my mom was right because we could hear him jumping around inside the wall that is right over the door of

Madam's fancy bathroom that has the morning glory wallpaper and the old-time bathtub with golden faucets. And my mom said, "I think he fell in and is stuck there because I doubt there is any way for him to go up or out."

So I ran down the back stairs to the kitchen and pulled on Pop's arm and said, "Hurry, Pop. Jake needs you upstairs."

But Pop said, "Children first."

Then he pushed the screwdriver underneath the dumbwaiter door and banged it with the hammer until it made a sound like SWAK and flew open. But inside the dumbwaiter looked empty except for rope. And then I was scared. "Don't tell me we've lost him, too," I said to Pop.

But Pop pulled on the rope and up came the dumbwaiter and out came Melonhead. I NEVER thought I'd be glad to see him but actually I was. Very. Then I asked him, "Were you scared?"

And he said, "I had the time of my life."

So Melonhead and I took the chisel and the hammer but left the crows bar because we did not need it Pop said and went all up to the bathroom and my mom showed Pop where she thought

Jake was trapped and Madam got a chair for Pop to stand on and Mom got a shoe box from Madam's closet. Then Pop said, "I need room. Everybody has to stand in the bathtub except for Lucy Rose because she is my assistant and it's her job to hold the box."

Then Pop stood on the chair and put the bathroom cup sideways on the wall and put his ear on the bottom of it so he could listen. "Something is in there and I hope it's a guinea pig," he said.

Then he took the chisel and the hammer and started tapping out a hole in the wall that was about as big as an Oreo and when he finished he said, "Someone give me some guinea pig food."

We all turned to Melonhead but all he said was, "Oops!"

It turned out that while he was stuck in the dumbwaiter he was feeling like he was hungry so he ate Jake's food which even my mom said was so gross but he said, "It wasn't so bad. It tasted sort of like oatmeal, if you mixed sand in it."

Then he said he found some dried apricots and he ate them, too.

"Man-o-man," I said. But I decided I wouldn't

tell him how those apricots had been in there for extremely long.

Jonique climbed out of the bathtub and ran down the back stairs to the kitchen and took the first food she could find which was one of Madam's soy bars and brought it back up. Pop broke a piece off and held it by the hole and we all were quiet for the longest time and then I made some little kissing noises and Jake's head came right through.

But his body did not. The hole Pop made was too small so Jake was stuck. And do you know how deer heads look on the wall? He was looking like a little guinea pig head hanging over the bathroom door which made us all laugh, especially me because I was so glad to see him.

The bad thing was that Pop had to push him back inside the wall so he could cut the hole bigger.

Then, finally, the hole was big enough and Pop reached in and got out Jake who was one dusty guinea pig eating a soy bar. Pop handed Jake down to me to put in the shoe box but first I kissed him right on his fur. A few minutes later, when Jake was in the box and we were all petting him, Madam

said, "Lucy Rose, you will have to paint me a really great picture that we can put in one of the frames and hang over the hole because I am never going to be able to find another roll of that wallpaper again."

And I said, "It will be a picture of Jake's head."

And then I was feeling even more thankful than at Thanksgiving and I turned to Adam Melon and said, "You are one good friend, Melonhead!"

And I don't know how that Melonhead part came out but he looked like he was feeling shocked plus hurt plus angry. And he said, "What did you call me?"

And I wanted to tell the biggest lie ever in my life but I didn't because of being honorable. Instead I told him, "I said Melonhead but I mean it in a nice way," which I figured out I did.

And he said, "Same with me when I called you a fart."

And we both laughed and mine was with relief.

MAY

May 1

I am feeling a little yuck about going back to school so I wrote to "Dear Lucy Rose": "What is the best way to tell something you would rather not say? A Nervous Person."

May 2

This is the answer I got: "Dear Nervous Person, Just say it."

May 4

Today, we went back to school and I still did not want to confess to Mr. Welsh about Jake's big adventure which is what my mom kept calling it but I was pretty sure it was the honorable thing. Besides Jonique said that if we didn't Melonhead probably would because even though he is pretty much our friend now he is the kind who has to tell everything. So I went to Mr. Welsh and I said, "I was not so responsible as I said I would be in my letter."

And he said, "How's that, Lucy Rose?"

So I told him the whole story and I said, "I learned a hard lesson and that is that I will not take him out again, especially without being much more careful about closing doors and maybe putting him in a box or something, if you let me keep him for some of the time in the summer."

And Mr. Welsh said something that I did not think he would which was, "This has happened to other kids before because the thing about Jake is that he is the sort of guinea pig you want to take out of the cage and when you do a lot of times he gets away."

When I told him about the dumbwaiter he said, "Well, you were resourceful, at least."

And when I told him about Adam Melon trying to save the day for me, Mr. Welsh said, "How about that?"

And he made a smile.

May 8

I e-mailed my father about one big thing I really need and it is a secret and I am waiting for the answer.

May 12

Our class went to the zoo to see Mr. Welsh's friend in Small Mammals and my mom and Mr. McBee came with us. Mr. McBee did have to tell Melonhead to shape up when we were riding on the subway and he was acting wild. But after we got back to school Melonhead's mom was waiting at the playground and she gave us one dollar so we could all go to Grubb's for a treat and Melonhead let Jonique and me decide and we picked Starburst. I try to not call him Melonhead in front of his mother.

May 18

Today I got a package from my dad and I took it to my room so I could open it in privacy and it is exactly the thing I need.

May 25

Since it's the last day of the year Jonique and Melonhead and I all walked to school together without any parents because that is one thing you can do when you are a fourth grader which we practically are. Jonique brought Mr. Welsh zucchini bread that was made by herself and Mrs. McBee, and Melonhead brought him a $10 gift card from the Politics and Prose bookstore and I brought a red bag but I was not wanting to tell what's in it until later.

At school we ate donuts and we packed up our lockers and got our report cards and was I ever surprised because Mrs. Washburn wrote the comment of "Reading and classroom behavior are much improved."

Then at the last minute of the last day, I gave Mr. Welsh the red bag and a card made by me. And this is what the card said:

Dear Mr. Welsh,
This is for you. You don't have to eat it.

Love,
Lucy Rose

And he gave me an oddball look and reached right in and got out his present which was a baseball cap that has the Ann Arbor Aardvarks team on the front of it.

"I love it," Mr. Welsh said and he tried it on. And it fit perfectly.

"It came by FedEx," I told him. "It's from my dad's school."

"You know, I've been needing a hat," he said.

"I figured that out," I told him.

"I'm glad your year got better, Lucy Rose," Mr. Welsh said.

"First it got better and then it got mostly good and now it's pretty great, actually."

"Do you still want to go back to Ann Arbor?" Mr. Welsh asked me.

"For visiting," I told him. "But not for keeps."

May 27

I was almost asleep when I thought of something and I got up and ran down to the kitchen and I turned on the computer and I typed a new e-mail and here is what it said: "Dear Lucy Rose, Thank you for all the advice. Signed, The Person Who Has Your Same Name."

And the answer came back right away: "Dear Person Who Has My Same Name, Was I any help? Love, Madam."

"Sometimes," I wrote back. "Did you always know it was me?"

"Yes," Madam wrote.

"How?" I asked her back.

"How could I not?" she said. "You are my dear Lucy Rose."

That gave me a good feeling.

"And," she said, "I know your and your mom's e-mail address."

I had never thought of that.

May 30

This morning my mom and I had a fruit plate breakfast at Jimmy T's for the first Sunday of summer and on the walk home my mom held my hand and she said, "A lot has changed in one year, hasn't it?"

"Yep," I said. "For one thing, I used to be a suburb girl. Now I'm a city girl."

"That's true," my mom said.

"And I like it," I said.

"I'm glad," she told me.

"And I made a true friend," I said.

"That's very valuable," my mom said.

"And I made a friend from my enemy," I said.

"That's quite important," she told me.

"And I learned about telling the truth."

"Extremely important," my mom said.

"And I figured out that sometimes things that seem bad work out okay," I said.

"Like Daddy and me being separated?" she asked me.

"Exactly like that," I said.

Then we walked for a block and I remembered some more things. "I learned to e-mail," I said.

"That's useful," my mom told me.

"And to sing most of the songs from *The Music Man*."

"That's entertaining," my mom said to me.

"And to refinish," I said.

"Lucky for me," she said.

"And to be responsible, at least when I am taking care of a guinea pig," I told her.

"And I learned to like a guinea pig," my mom said.

"That's important," I told her.

Then she said, "You should be proud of yourself, Lucy Rose."

And I said, "I am one person who agrees with that."

May 31, Memorial Day

Tonight we had a cookout in Madam and Pop's backyard and Mrs. McBee brought green Jell-O salad with baby marshmallows to go with Madam's soyburgers and Mrs. Melon brought corn on the cob and my mom brought the greatest thing which was chicken fingers. We all had sidewalk sundaes even the grown-ups and Mr. McBee went wild with the hose afterwards and when it was all dark and we were sitting on the porch watching for fireflies Pop told Melonhead, "I have a good summer job for you."

And Melonhead said, "What is it?"

And Pop said, "We need to clean the chimney and the only way I can think to do that is to tie a rope around a small boy's ankles and lower him down from the roof."

And Melonhead said, "All right!"

And then Madam looked at Pop with those Madam eyes she has and we all laughed our heads off except for Mrs. Melon who only laughed a little.

When the McBees were leaving, Jonique and I made a deal that we would go straight to the Parks & Rec center the first minute it opens for summer so I could learn to make a gimp key chain for my mom's birthday and Jonique could make a pot holder because she always has wanted to.

And then, while we were waving goodbye to the McBees, Melonhead reached in his pocket and pulled out a little piece of paper and gave it to me and he said, "This is a present for you and your grandmother."

We looked at it and it said: MADAM I'M ADAM.

I was thinking it was one crummy present but Madam was smiling like crazy.

"Read it backwards," Melonhead said.

I did and I couldn't believe it.